Gargoylz

at a Midnight Feast

Gargoylz: grotesque stone creatures found on old buildings, spouting rainwater from the guttering. Sometimes seen causing mischief and mayhem before scampering away over rooftops.

Read all the
Gargoylz adventures!

Gargoylz on the Loose!

Gargoylz Get Up to Mischief

Gargoylz at a Midnight Feast

Gargoylz Take a Trip

Gargoylz

at a Midnight Feast

Burchett & Vogler

illustrated by Leighton Noyes

RED FOX

GARGOYLZ AT A MIDNIGHT FEAST
A RED FOX BOOK 978 1 862 30866 4

First published in Great Britain by Red Fox,
an imprint of Random House Children's Books
A Random House Group Company

This edition published 2009

1 3 5 7 9 10 8 6 4 2

Series created and developed by Amber Caravéo
Copyright © Random House Children's Books, 2009

The Random House Group Limited supports the Forest Stewardship
Council (FSC), the leading international forest certification organization.
All our titles that are printed on Greenpeace-approved FSC-certified paper
carry the FSC logo. Our paper procurement policy can be found at
www.rbooks.co.uk/environment

Set in Bembo Schoolbook

Red Fox Books are published by Random House Children's Books,
61–63 Uxbridge Road, London W5 5SA

www.**kids**at**randomhouse**.co.uk
www.**rbooks**.co.uk

Addresses for companies within The Random House Group Limited can be
found at: www.randomhouse.co.uk/offices.htm

THE RANDOM HOUSE GROUP Limited Reg. No. 954009

A CIP catalogue record for this book is available from the British Library.

Printed and bound in Great Britain by CPI Bookmarque, Croydon, CR0 4TD

For Emily Groome, with love. *Auntie Sara*
- **Burchett & Vogler**

For my Nephew Hayden, who's a bit like Ben
- **Leighton Noyes**

Hello, I'm the Web Gargoyle.
Look out for me – I'll be hiding in one
of the pictures in the book.
When you spot me, be sure to make a
note of the secret codeword I'm holding.
The codeword unlocks a secret level
of the amazing Gargoylz game
on our fabulous website at
www.gargolyz.co.uk

Oldacre Primary School

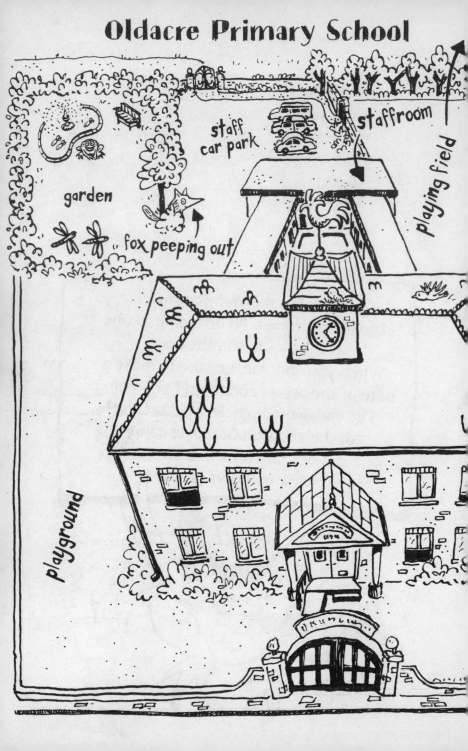

staff car park

staffroom

playing field

garden

fox peeping out

playground

St Mark's Church

playground

School Report - Max Black

Days absent: 0

Days late: 0

Max is a bright boy. If he spent as much time on his school work as he does on annoying Lucinda Tellingly he would get much better marks. I am pleased to see that he enjoys exercise - although I do not count running down corridors making racing car noises. Also I would be glad if he did not shout "Awesome" quite so loudly every time we have football practice.

Class teacher - Miss Deirdre Bleet

The only good thing I can say about Max Black is that he is always early for school. However, he is the last one into the classroom. He spends far too much time playing tricks with Ben Neal. Mrs Pumpkin is still off sick after discovering an earwig farm in her handbag. Max ignores all school rules. He has recently developed a curious interest in drainpipes and has been seen talking to the wall. This behaviour is outrageous and must stop.

Head teacher - Hagatha Hogsbottom (Mrs)

School Report - Ben Neal

Days absent: 0

Days late: 0

Ben has many abilities which he does not always use. He works very hard at dreaming up tricks to play, which gives him very little time to concentrate on his learning. He enjoys football and skateboarding - indeed, he and his board can frequently be found upside down in a flowerbed.

Class teacher - Miss Deirdre Bleet

Ben Neal is a strange boy. He is often to be found grinning at gutters.

He constantly breaks school rule number 742: boys must not break school rules.

Ben thinks he can get away with anything by flashing his blue eyes and looking innocent. I am not fooled. Indeed I am still waiting for him and Max Black to write a note of apology to Mr Bucket the caretaker. Gluing his wellington boots to the staffroom ceiling was outrageous!

Head teacher - Hagatha Hogsbottom (Mrs)

Contents

1. Sports Day Mischief   1

2. Barney Cooks Up a Storm   33

3. Secret Plan: Free Theo   61

4. Midnight Feast Fun   89

1. Sports Day Mischief

Max Black and his best friend, Ben Neal, nine-year-old super secret agents, were on their way to school. They had an important mission.

"Ready for action, Agent Neal?" asked Max.

Ben nodded. "Ready, Agent Black."

Max bent down and tied his right leg tightly to Ben's left with his school scarf. He straightened up. "We're sure to win the three-legged race at Sports Day after all this practice. Go!"

The boys lurched forwards, wobbled

and fell over.

"Better sort out our technique if we're going to break the world record," said Ben, rubbing his knee.

"Let's try again," said Max as they staggered to their feet. "The starter has raised his pistol . . . wait for it . . . **BANG**!"

They bounded off down the road, this time without a stumble.

Max's spy radar picked up someone in the distance: pale, skinny, frilly socks. He knew what that meant. It was Enemy Agent Lucinda Tellingly, codename: Bossy Boots.

They whizzed past her, making her ponytail fly.

"You don't stand a chance!" she called after them nastily.

Ben twisted round to stick his tongue out and fell into a hedge, taking Max with him. Lucinda cackled loudly.

"She'll be sorry when we beat her and the rest of Year Four," said Max, pulling leaves out of his spiky dark hair.

They untangled themselves and belted off again at breakneck speed.

"Awesome pacc!" panted Ben. "I can't

wait for this afternoon. Sports Day's the best day of the school year, apart from Christmas Dinner Day."

"Every school day's cool now we've got our secret friends," said Max.

They reached the gates of Oldacre Primary and flung their arms round the gatepost to stop. Max peered up at the ancient church next door. The gutters and spouts were decorated with carved gargoylz. Only Max and Ben knew that the little stone creatures were alive and loved to play tricks — just like the boys.

They made for the wall between the playground and the church.

"Greetingz," came a growly purr.

A gargoyle with a monkey face, big pointy ears and sparkling eyes was sitting on a gravestone in the churchyard. It was Toby.

"Dangling drainpipes!" he exclaimed. "Two headz? Three legz? Have you turned

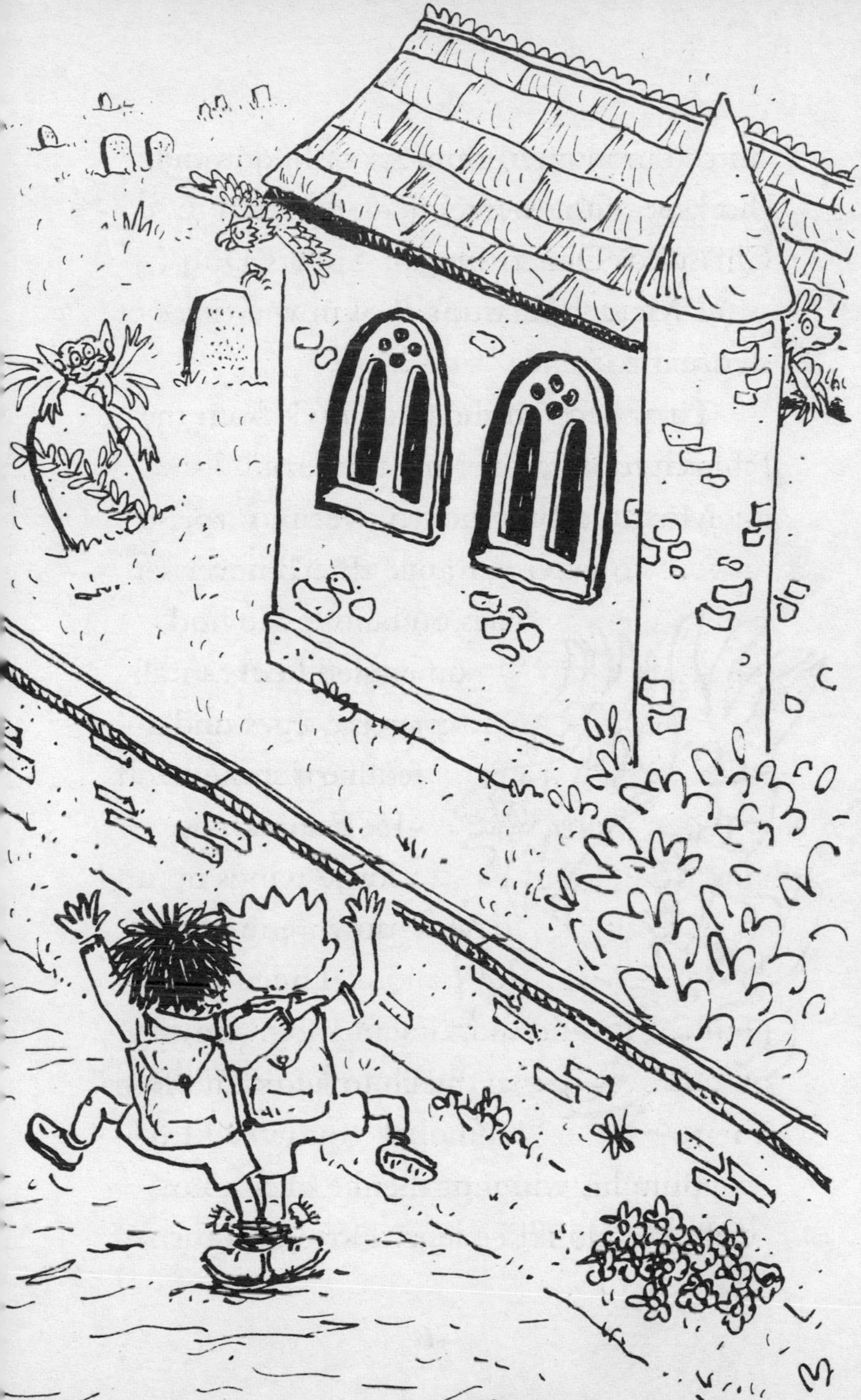

into a monster? I thought only gargoylz
had special powerz."

"We're practising for Sports Day,"
said Max. "We want to win the three-
legged race."

They heard a sharp squawk from the
church roof. "Shiver me timbers!"

Max and Ben looked over in surprise
to see a gargoyle they'd never set
eyes on before. He had
an eagle's beak, small
piercing eyes and a
feathery stone head.
He flapped his
large wings up and
down eagerly.

"This is Ira,"
said Toby. "Ira, say
hello to Max and Ben."

"Humanz!" squawked Ira,
flapping his wings at them. "Make 'em
walk the plank!"

"I've told you about Max and Ben,"
said Toby patiently. "They're our friendz."

"Part of the crew?" asked Ira
suspiciously.

"Yes, they'll keep our secret," Toby
assured him. "They're almost as good
as gargoylz."

"Welcome aboard then," said Ira,
saluting with a wing.

"Why does he talk like that?" Ben
whispered to Toby.

"He's never been the same since a parrot from a pirate ship landed on him," explained Toby. "Now he thinks he's a pirate too."

"Outrageous!" came a shriek from across the playground.

Toby and Ira froze.

Max's radar burst into action: grey hair, beaky nose, evil eyes flashing. He knew what that meant. It was Enemy Agent Mrs Hogsbottom, commonly known as Mrs Hogsbum, codename: Evil Head Teacher.

Mrs Hogsbottom strode up to them, making the playground shake. "How dare you break school rule number eight hundred and forty-three: boys must not use their stripy school scarves to tie their legs together!"

"We're practising for the three-legged race this afternoon," Ben tried to explain.

"We want to break the world record," added Max.

"No excuses!" snapped Mrs Hogsbottom. She marched off and shouted at some girls who were singing too happily.

The gargoylz unfroze.

"Nasty old landlubber!" squawked Ira.

"I'd love to see you break the world record," said Toby wistfully.

"Why don't you come and watch?" suggested Max.

"We'll be on the school field all afternoon. You can hide in the hedge like you did last night when we played that trick on Science Club."

"Spluttering gutterz!" Toby grinned. "What a good idea. See you there."

* * *

It was a bright, sunny afternoon and
Sports Day started right after lunch.
Everything was ready.

When no one was looking, Max and Ben sidled over to the hedge and peered through the leaves. Seven pairs of stone eyes stared back at them.

"You've all come to watch," said Max. "Awesome!"

A dog-faced gargoyle with spines down his back smiled at them shyly. "Toby says you're going to break the world record."

"Too right, Barney," Ben told him. He looked over at the board of events. "Our race is last," he groaned. "That's ages."

"Time for a trick then," said Max.

The gargoylz gave a great cheer.

Max whipped a small pot out of his pocket. "This is the perfect way to get Lucinda back for being mean to us on the way to school. She's in the sack race next, with all her friends. Time for Secret Plan: Itchy Surprise."

Ben read the label aloud: "*Jimmy Joker's Best Itching Powder*. Just the thing, Agent Black. I can't wait to see Lucinda's face when she starts scratching. But how do we put it in the sacks without being seen?"

"Ssspluttering guttersss! That sounds like a trick for me to play." A gargoyle with a head covered with wriggling snakes grinned up at him.

"Brilliant plan, Eli," said Max, handing the pot to him. "Off you go."

Eli took the pot in his mouth, turned into a grass snake and slithered off towards the pile of brown sacks. He was soon back

Lucinda and the other racers climbed
into their sacks and stood eagerly at the
starting line.

"*I* haven't bothered to practise," Lucinda
said loudly, seeing Max and Ben watching.
"I'll win anyway."

"Ready, steady, **wheeeee**!" Mr Widget
blew the starting whistle. The race began.
The competitors bounced along the grass,

cheered on by their classmates. But one
by one they began to jump about wildly,
scratching all over. Max and Ben found it
hard to keep a straight face when Lucinda
shot out of her sack and ran off, shrieking.
Finally Mr Widget called the race off.

"OUTRAGEOUS!" bellowed Mrs Hogsbottom from her special head teacher's chair. "Give them all extra homework!"

There was a volley of gargoyle cackles from the hedge.

"Exsssellent!" declared Eli, the snakes on his head hissing in delight. "What a prank!"

"We haven't finished yet." Max grinned. "I've thought of a brilliant way to make our race come sooner. We'll speed up all the other races. What's next?"

"Infants' egg and spoon," Ben read from the board.

"Time for Secret Plan: Sticky Egg and Spoon Race," declared Max. He pulled a tube of glue from his pocket. "Follow me, Agent Neal. No one will see. They're all watching the trampolining." They sneaked over to where the special spoons and hard-boiled eggs were waiting for the infants' race.

"We'll stick every egg to a spoon," chuckled Max. "The infants won't have to wobble along for hours trying to balance them. It'll be the fastest egg and spoon race on the planet."

"Awesome plan, Agent Black," said Ben.

Max had just blobbed a drop of glue onto the first spoon when he heard a bellow. It was Mrs Hogsbottom.

"What do you think you're doing?"

"We're helping the little ones out," said Ben. "Making the race a bit easier for them." He put on his best innocent look. It always worked on the dinner ladies, who cooed over his blond hair and blue eyes and gave him extra baked beans. It never worked on Mrs Hogsbottom.

"Outrageous!" she growled, taking the glue and putting it in her pocket. "Trying to help someone cheat, were you?"

"Oh no," protested Max. "We were going to glue all of them the same."

Mrs Hogsbottom marched them over to their class. "Sit down quietly and wait for your race. And no more nonsense."

"*Nonsense?*" said Max indignantly when she'd stomped back to her chair. "We were being helpful. She could at least have said thank you."

"No chance," said Ben. "It's probably against one of her school rules." He looked over to where the obstacle race was just finishing. "It's our turn soon," he said excitedly. "Let's practise."

They charged along to their teacher, Miss Bleet.

"Can we have our leg tie, please, miss?" asked Ben. "We're running together."

"I can't possibly let you do that!" she said nervously. "You'll do something silly. I've not forgotten last year when you put flour bombs in the long jump sand."

"But we have to run together," pleaded Max. "We're going to break the world record."

"The world record will have to wait," insisted Miss Bleet. "I have a better idea. Something that will keep you out of trouble. Ben, you'll be Tiffany's partner, and Max, you go with Lucinda."

Max and Ben gawped at their teacher.

"You can't mean—" spluttered Max.

"Tied to girls!" groaned Ben. "And not just *any* girls – Lucinda and Tiffany are the most goody-goody girls in the history of goody-goody girls!"

"They smell all flowery, miss," Max told her earnestly. "We'll die from the pong and it'll be your fault."

Miss Bleet waved him away.

Max's face suddenly lit up.

"It's Friday," he hissed happily in Ben's ear. "And it's nearly three o'clock."

Ben stared at him. "How's that going to stop us being trapped with the ghastly girls?"

Max beamed. "My sister goes to gym at the sports centre on Fridays after school. I had to promise to be ready at three so that Mum could pick us both up and get Jessica there in time." He peered at the crowd of spectators to find his mum. "She'll be waving at me any minute to say it's time to go. We're saved."

"You're forgetting one thing," said Ben miserably. "*You* might be saved but I'm not. I'm going to be tied to Tiffany Goodchild. My life is over."

"I'd forgotten that." Max frowned. "We need a special plan for you."

"Got it!" said Ben. "I'll tell Miss Bleet I've broken my leg. I can't race then."

"Excellent plan, Agent Neal," said Max. "I'll let Mum know I'm ready to go while you break the news to Miss Bleet."

Ben ran off.

"Don't forget to limp!" Max yelled after him.

Three minutes later Ben was back. Max was sitting by the hedge, his head in his hands.

"I can't believe my idea didn't work!" he groaned. "Nan's taking Jessica to gym so that Mum can watch us break the world record."

"And Miss Bleet didn't believe I'd broken my leg," said Ben sadly. "Even when I collapsed in front of her and rolled about like a footballer. Now we're doomed to be tied to those smelly girls."

"What's wrong?" said a gurgly voice. Toby popped up between them.

They told him all about the terrible fate that awaited them.

Toby smiled. "Perhaps

we could help. There must be one of our special powerz that will work."

"Awesome," said Max, cheering up. "But which one?"

Toby scratched his stony chin. "My flying won't be much use."

"And Barney's stinky smells don't work on people outdoors unless they're really close to him," said Ben.

Toby's golden eyes suddenly lit up. "We need Zack!" he declared. "Zack can make himself invisible and steal those red things Miss Bleet is going to tie your legs with."

"Perfect!" exclaimed Max. "No ties, no race. But where *is* Zack?"

POP! Zack appeared out of nowhere. He ran up and down the grass, tail swishing eagerly. "Did someone call?" he panted.

Max quickly explained what they wanted him to do. **POP!** Zack vanished. In an instant he was back, some red ties in his mouth and some draped over his fuzzy mane. Ben shoved them under the hedge and covered them with leaves.

"Take your places for the three-legged race," trumpeted Mrs Hogsbottom.

"Let's go." Max grinned. "We'd better look keen."

Miss Bleet tripped off to find the ties and the boys ran over to stand next to their partners. Lucinda scowled at Max.

Max smiled sweetly back. Any minute now
their teacher would find there weren't any
ties and the race would be abandoned.

But now Miss Bleet was approaching
– holding some ropes. The boys gawped at
her in horror.

"Couldn't find the ties,"
she twittered nervously.
"But these will do
just as well."

"Help!" Max
groaned as she
tied him to his
partner. "I'll catch
the Lucinda Lurgy
being this close!"

"Shut up, horrible
boy!" snapped Lucinda.

Ben tried to twist himself free from
Tiffany. "I'm being overcome by
dangerous girly fumes!" he gasped.

But it was too late. Mr Widget was

starting the race. "Ready ... steady ..."

Suddenly the sky went dark and huge drops of rain began to fall, faster and faster.

In seconds everyone was soaked to the skin.

"Outrageous!" bellowed Mrs Hogsbottom, putting up a huge black umbrella and not letting anyone share it. "School rule number four hundred and thirteen – it must *not* rain on Sports Day! Everybody inside. At the double!"

Lucinda gave a loud shriek and turned to run back into school with everyone else. But she'd forgotten she was still tied to Max. She took one step and fell face down in a puddle.

Trying not to laugh too loudly, Max and Ben hurried to undo their ropes and help Lucinda up. By the time they'd hauled her to her feet she was covered from head to foot in cold wet mud.

"Shame," giggled Ben as they watched her squelching across the grass with Tiffany. "Not our fault if a bit of extra mud accidentally got wiped all over her."

Max spotted Toby beckoning from the hedge and ran over through the teeming rain. Ben followed him across the grass. The gargoylz had big grins on their stone faces. Zack was rolling over and over, giggling helplessly.

Toby gave them a thumbs-up. "Good trick on Lucinda," he chortled. "I haven't laughed so much since we put the vicar's Harvest Festival display on the roof."

"And that rain came just at the right moment," said Max. "What luck!"

"That wasn't luck," said Toby. "That was Ira's special power."

"Ira can make it rain?" gasped Ben in amazement. "Awesome!"

"Only in short bursts," explained Toby.

"But for long enough to save us," said Max. "Thanks, Ira."

"Anything for a shipmate!" squawked Ira, saluting them from the hedge.

The rain stopped as suddenly as it had started. Ben wrung out his T-shirt. "We'd better go back to school," he said.

"See you again soon, gargoylz," Max called into the hedge. "This has been the best Sports Day ever!"

2. Barney Cooks Up a Storm

Max and Ben whirred through the school gates in their imaginary spy helicopter.

"Secret Mission: Spot the Gargoylz!" whispered Max, chugging to a halt.

"Right away, Agent Black." Ben put his hands up to his eyes like binoculars and scanned the church roof. "No sign of them. Not even a tail."

"Try the churchyard," suggested Max.

The boys zoomed across to the wall between Oldacre School and the church next door. They peered over. Five stony

shapes were huddled together in the long
grass.

Max's spy radar whirred into action:
small, cheeky, full of tricks. He knew what
that meant. It was their secret friends, the
gargoylz.

Toby's head popped up from the
huddle. "Greetingz!" he called across in
a doleful voice. He flew onto the wall
next to the boys. Barney, Theo, Eli and
Zack scrambled up to join him. The five
gargoylz sat in a row, their tails drooping.

"What's wrong?" asked Max, looking at
their mournful faces. "You haven't run out
of pranks, have you?"

Toby shook his head. "Of course not!" he exclaimed. "That could never happen. We're just worried about Bart. You know he's always a bit grumpy . . ."

"Well, lately he's got worse . . ." Theo told the boys, his tiger ears flopping sadly.

"And now he's really missssserable," hissed Eli.

"We're trying to find a way to stop him being so down in the dumps," said Barney.

"Bounce on him?" suggested Zack, jumping up and down on his big floppy feet.

"That would probably make him grumpier than ever," laughed Max. "But there must be something we can do."

"I've got an idea!" Ben said suddenly. "Max is coming for a sleepover on

Friday night. Why don't you all come too? If you bring Bart we could give him a surprise party!"

The gargoylz looked puzzled.

"What's a sleepover?" asked Toby, scratching his stony head with one claw.

"It's when you sleep at a friend's house," explained Max. "Only you don't sleep much – you stay up really late and have a midnight feast and play games and tell stories! It's awesome!"

Toby's golden eyes lit up. "Dangling drainpipes!" he shouted. "That'll be just the thing for Bart!"

The spikes on Barney's back quivered happily and Zack jumped over Theo's head in excitement. Suddenly they all heard menacing footsteps clomping across the playground towards them. The gargoylz froze into statues.

Max activated his spy radar: grey hair, beaky nose, teeth like a crocodile. It was Enemy Agent Mrs Hogsbottom, commonly known as Mrs Hogsbum, codename: Evil Head Teacher. She had come halfway across the playground and now stopped to shout at the boys.

The gargoylz sat on the wall with frozen grins.

"School rule number three hundred and fifty-nine," yelled Mrs Hogsbottom, "boys must not put ugly stone things on school walls. Get rid of them and go to your classroom. Immediately!" She stomped off again towards her office.

"Who's she calling ugly?" protested Toby. "Her face could crack mirrors!"

"I don't think she's ever looked in a mirror," said Ben. "She'd frighten herself to death."

Max heard Mrs Hogsbum's office window opening. "Better go," he hissed. "See you later."

The boys sped off into school. When Max turned at the door and looked back, the gargoylz had gone.

"Miss Bleet's in the worst mood in the history of worst moods," muttered Max as he and Ben sat in class after play, chewing their pencils.

"Too right," agreed Ben. "Every time I read my comic instead of my English book she tells me off! Weird!"

"And when we were looking out of the window at Barney earlier she got really cross," said Max. "We told her it was important but she wouldn't listen."

"I wonder what Barney was doing running across the playground anyway," said Ben. "He had a piece of paper in his paw."

"It must have been important," said Max. "He was in such a hurry."

"Max and Ben," quavered Miss Bleet, "please stop chattering! I am having a very bad morning and you're making it worse!" She dabbed at her forehead with her hankie.

"What's wrong, miss?" asked Ben.

"There was no sugar for my coffee," she told them grumpily. "None! It's disappeared. I can't get through the morning without coffee and I can't drink coffee without sugar – especially with you two in the class!"

"I've had something go missing too," piped up Tiffany. "My chocolate bar wasn't in my bag at playtime."

"Nor was mine," called Duncan.

"And my Chocomunch had vanished from my pocket when I looked for it," declared Lucinda loudly. "It was a specially big one."

Several other voices joined in until there was a clamour of complaints around the classroom.

"That's enough!" exclaimed Miss Bleet, clutching her head. "You'll just have to manage without. I'll look into it later. Now, get on with your work."

The two boys looked at each other.

"We're the only ones who didn't have their snacks pinched," Ben whispered to

Max. "I wonder why."

"Something very strange is going on in this school," Max whispered back. "We've got a new secret mission, Agent Neal. We must find the missing sugar and chocolate."

"Agreed, Agent Black," answered Ben. "After lunch though. It's jam sponge for pudding today. My favourite!"

"No jam sponge!" exclaimed Ben as he and Max stood at the hatch at lunch time.

"I don't believe it."

"Sorry, dear, but we couldn't make any today," Mrs Coddle the dinner lady told him. "The eggs have all disappeared. Every single one. We'll make one tomorrow. You'll have to have an apple for now." She plonked one down on Ben's plate.

Ben looked up at her with pleading blue eyes.

"Oh, you poor thing," she said, and fetched him a banana to go with it.

Max's eyes narrowed. "Our mission has changed, Agent Neal," he muttered as the boys mooched off to find a table. "There's a food thief in school – someone who likes sugar, chocolate and eggs – and it's our job to find out who it is."

As soon as they had finished their lunch, the boys ran out into the playground.

"Let's snoop around for a bit," said Max. "See if we can find a hoard of stolen food."

They sneaked about, holding imaginary magnifying glasses and trying to spot someone with a pocket full of chocolate bars.

"What's this?" Max said suddenly. There was a pile of chocolate wrappers by the staffroom window. "Is the thief one of the teachers?" He peered through the window at the teachers, who were having their lunch. No one was eating chocolate. Then a foil wrapper fluttered down from the roof. Max and Ben looked up. Barney was sitting in the gutter – covered in sticky brown goo!

"What are you up to?" asked Max curiously.

Barney went red under his goo. "I'm making chocolate chip cookiez for the midnight feast," he explained shyly. He produced a bowl and spoon and flapped

a piece of paper. "I got this recipe from the vicar's cookery book. Then I . . . er . . . found some sugar and eggs and chocolate." He licked his lips. "Chocolate," he sighed. "Yum!"

Max and Ben looked at each other.

"So the mystery of the food thief is solved!" Max whispered to Ben. "Great idea, Barney," he called up, "but how are you going to cook the cookies?"

There was a small roar from the roof and Max and Ben jumped in alarm as a long flame suddenly flickered over the guttering.

"Don't worry," Barney told them. "That's just my friend Azzan. Come and say hello, Azzan."

A dragon-like gargoyle with scaly skin and a long swishing tail poked his head over the edge of the roof.

"Humanz!" he cried in alarm, opening his mouth and taking a huge breath.

Barney quickly reached out a paw and clamped his jaws shut.

"No more fire, Azzan!" he said, looking worried. "These are our friends. We don't want to frazzle them."

"I'm baking the cookiez," said Azzan proudly when Barney finally let go.

"You know my special power is making smellz," Barney told the boys. "Well, Azzan's is breathing fire."

"That's great!" said Ben, wide-eyed in amazement.

"There's only one problem," Barney explained. "Azzan's fire doesn't last very long and he can't always control it – a bit like me and my smellz. Some of my cooking got a tiny bit burned." He scuttled off and came back with a tray. It was covered in smouldering black cookies.

"It's OK." Azzan grinned. "We've got plenty more ingredients. Come and look."

Max and Ben scrambled onto a nearby dustbin so that they could see onto the

roof. The dragony gargoyle was pushing
his nose into a pile of chocolate bars,
sugar and boxes of eggs. A little flame
suddenly shot out of his mouth and set
fire to one of the boxes.

"Ooops!" Azzan cried, and jumped up
and down on it. By the time the flames
had gone out he was knee-deep in egg
yolk. "Never mind," he said chirpily.
"Plenty more where they came from."

"You've got about sixty eggs there!"
exclaimed Max. "You won't need all those
for the cookies."

"Won't we?" said Barney. "Oh dear.

What shall we do with them?"

"We must give some back to the dinner ladies," said Ben, looking worried. "Otherwise they won't be able to make their yummy jam sponge tomorrow."

"Tell you what," said Max, "we'll take the eggs you don't need – that's most of them – back to the kitchen."

"But what if someone sees you?" protested Barney anxiously as he and Azzan carefully handed the boxes of eggs down to the boys. "Theo nearly got caught by a human waving a big ladle when he was getting them for me."

"Good point," said Max, scratching his head for a moment. "Got it! Azzan, we'll need your help with a trick. You just have to sneak in through that door there and breathe some flames onto the fire detector – that's the round white thing on the ceiling in the corridor. That'll make the alarm go off and everyone will think there's a fire and leave the building."

"And we'll put the eggs back while the dinner ladies are out in the playground!" finished Ben. "Brilliant idea, Agent Black!"

"A prank! A prank! We're going to do a prank!" chanted Barney. A terrible pong filled the air.

"Barney's done a bottom burp!" wheezed Azzan in delight, sending a small burst of sparks dancing across the roof.

Clutching the egg boxes, Max and Ben sneaked off behind the bins that stood next to the kitchen window. From there they watched Azzan shin down the drainpipe and slip in through the nearest door. A few seconds later – **clang! clang! clang!** – a loud alarm bell rang out across the school.

Azzan scampered back to the roof and
soon everyone was pouring out of the
buildings into the playground, shrieking
and yelling. The dinner ladies burst out
of the kitchen, carrying dishcloths and
wooden spoons.

SECRET CODEWORD:
JOKE

"Go, go, go!" Agent Black cried. "The kitchen should be empty now."

The two boys slipped in through the window. Suddenly a door opened on the other side of the room. They dived down behind a counter and squeezed onto a shelf between a sausage-making machine and a giant teapot.

Max's spy radar whirred into action: stout legs, white overall, strong smell of mashed potato. He knew what that meant. It was Mrs Simmer, chief cook, codename: Manic Masher. She marched towards the boys' hiding place.

"There's a fire," they heard her mutter. "I must rescue my potato masher!"

Max and Ben held their breath as Mrs
Simmer's footsteps went past them. She
opened a drawer above their heads, took
something out and then hurried off into
the playground.

"I thought she was never going
to leave," said Ben. "I was dead
uncomfortable. I was sitting on the
teapot spout."

"She shouldn't have hung around," said
Max disapprovingly as the boys crawled
out of their hiding place. "She could've
got burned."

"It wasn't a real fire," Ben reminded him.

"Yeah, but she didn't know that," insisted Max.

Ben nodded in agreement. "Grown-ups are idiots."

They put the eggs on the counter, high-fived and raced to join their class, just as Miss Bleet was calling the register.

After school Max and Ben tore out into the playground.

"Can't wait to see how Barney's cookies are coming on," said Ben. "He should have made plenty by now."

"Hope he lets us try one," said Max. "Look, he's over there on the church roof."

They ran into the churchyard and
peered up at the porch. Barney was
clutching a large bowl and trying to stop
Toby and Azzan dipping their paws in it.
A runny brown mixture
slopped over the rim.

"Hey, Barney,"
called Max.
"How's the
cooking going?"

"Not very well,
I'm afraid," Barney
admitted sadly.
"Toby put too much
butter in one batch,
Azzan set fire to the next lot and this is my
last bowlful. I'm *not* going to let anything
happen to it."

He held it out to show the boys. As he
did, there was a **POP!** and Zack suddenly
appeared out of thin air, racing up the wall
of the church.

"Where are the cookiez?" he yelled, springing eagerly onto the porch and landing in the middle of the gargoylz. The bowl of cookie mixture was knocked clean out of Barney's paws and flew up into the air. **Splat!** It landed upside down on Barney's head, and Max and Ben and the gargoylz were all covered in sticky chocolate goo.

For a moment there was silence. Then everyone burst out laughing.

"Spluttering gutterz!" gasped Toby. "I haven't had such fun since Azzan ran along the washing line and singed the vicar's knickers!"

Barney pushed the mixing bowl off his head and it tumbled over the edge of the roof. Ben caught it.

"Don't know why I bothered trying to cook this," Barney said, licking his lips as his friends started slurping up the spilled cookie mixture. "It's delicious as it is!"

Max and Ben dipped their fingers into the bowl and tried a bit for themselves.

"You're right!" declared Max with a grin.

"It's scrumptious!" Ben agreed.

And then everyone was too busy slurping to say anything else at all.

3. Secret Plan: Free Theo

It was Friday evening. Secret Agent Max Black sped along the pavement in his imaginary spy motor boat with a top secret cargo in his rucksack. He had to get to fellow Agent Ben Neal's headquarters without delay.

He swerved to a halt at Ben's front door.

"Can I get out now?" came a grumpy voice from the rucksack. "That was a very uncomfortable ride."

"Sorry, Bart," Max whispered over his shoulder as he rang the bell. "But you'll have to wait a bit longer. Someone might

spot you here — and you know gargoylz
mustn't be seen by humans."

"Hmmph!" came the cross reply.
"Where are we anyway?"

"Can't tell you," said Max. "But I think
you'll like it."

Bart had been extra grumpy recently
so Max, Ben and the other gargolyz had
arranged a surprise sleepover to
cheer him up.

The front
door opened.

"Hello, Max,"
said Ben's mum,
showing him in. "Ben's
in his room. Go on up."

Max leaped up the stairs and
knocked on Ben's bedroom door.

"Top secret delivery, Agent Neal," he
whispered.

The door opened a little and Ben's
beaming face could be seen through the
gap. "Is the coast clear, Agent Black?"
he asked.

"Clear," answered Max. Ben let him in.

Max opened his rucksack. "About time too," grumbled Bart, climbing out and straightening his gladiator's skirt. "I don't enjoy being shaken about like a—"

Bart stopped and his pointed ears shot up in amazement. He was in a bedroom, and there in front of him, in a grinning row on the bed, sat Toby, Zack, Eli and Barney.

"Sleepover surprise at Ben's house!" yelled the gargoylz.

"Spluttering gutterz!" exclaimed Bart.

"How did you all get here?"

Toby grinned, his golden eyes flashing. "I flew all the way."

"I came in Ben's rucksack after school," added Barney.

"I turned into a sssnake and ssslithered here," Eli told him. "I made the girl in next door's garden ssscream," he added. The snakes on his head giggled at this in a hissy sort of way.

"I was invisible," said Zack, bouncing on the bed and knocking the other gargoylz over. "Well – most of the time."

"Everyone's going to sleep here tonight," Ben told Bart. "We're going to have fun. Here's our midnight feast." He pulled a huge chocolate cake

and a bottle of fizzy drink from under the bed. The gargoylz sat up, tongues hanging out. "It's going to be awesome."

"Is it?" said Bart doubtfully.

"And I've brought cookies!" said Max, taking a tin out of his rucksack. "Jessica made them with Mum – and gave some to me! Can't think what came over her."

"Cookiez and cake. Cookiez and cake!" shouted Zack excitedly, bounding about the bedroom.

"Everyone's here," said Barney eagerly. "Let's start the feast now."

"Feasts are silly," said Bart.

The other gargoylz dived for the cake.

"It's not midnight yet," said Ben, sliding it quickly back under the bed.

"Besides — anyone seen Theo?" asked Max, looking around.

"That's odd," said Eli. "He ssset off when I did. He changed into a kitten first, of courssse."

"He should be here by now then," said Max, puzzled.

"I'll go down and have a look outside," suggested Ben. "He might not remember which house to come to."

"Well, he is only four hundred and twelve," said Toby. "Young gargoylz aren't very good at directions."

Ben went off downstairs. In an instant he was back, a look of horror on his face.

"Arabella's got him!" he gasped. "My stupid sister thinks he's a real cat. She's made him a bed on the windowsill with a fluffy cushion and a blanket."

"We'll never get him back now!" said Bart grumpily.

"Course we will!" exclaimed Toby. "Gargoylz to the rescue!" He bounced off the bed and made for the door.

"You can't go down," Ben told him. "You'll be seen."

Toby's face fell.

"Don't worry," said Max. "I've got a plan – secret plan: Gargoyle Chain. Agent Neal, the sitting-room window is right under yours, correct?"

Ben nodded. "Correct, Agent Black."

"Then this is what we do," Max said. "You hold Barney's feet and dangle him out of the window, Barney holds Bart's feet,

Bart holds Toby's,
Toby holds Eli's and
Eli holds Zack's so that
Zack is at the bottom,
level with the sitting-
room window. A chain
of gargoylz!"

"Sounds dangerous,"
huffed Bart.

Ben grinned. "Will be
for me if Barney does a
bottom burp!"

"Sounds fun," said
Toby. "As good as a prank!"

Zack, Eli and Barney nodded in
agreement.

"Zack makes himself invisible so
Arabella doesn't see him," Max went on.
"Then he swings in through the window
and grabs Theo. Simple."

"And I haul them up to safety," finished
Ben. "Brilliant plan, Agent Black. But what
if Arabella sees Theo being whisked away?"

"She won't," said Max. "I'll go down
and cunningly distract her. When she finds

Theo's gone she'll just think he jumped
out of the window. It can't fail!" He strode
over to the door. "Wish me luck," he
said grimly. "I'm going into dangerous
territory."

Max peeped round the sitting-room door.
His radar went into overdrive: pigtails
bobbing, school badge gleaming, simpering
smile all over her face. He knew what that
meant. It was Enemy Agent Arabella Neal,

Codename:
Manic
monitor

SPY FILE:

Ben's sister, codename: Manic Monitor.

"What are you doing here?" said Arabella suspiciously when she saw him creep in. "Keep away from my new kitten."

"What a lovely little tabby!" Max managed to say, edging towards Theo, who was curled up in his bed, purring. "Where did you get it?"

"Poor Fluffikins was stuck up a tree," said Arabella. "He was so scared he was stiff as a statue. Now he needs to recover. So don't disturb him."

Max realized that Theo must have been on his way to the sleepover when he'd been surprised by a human – Arabella – though it was hard to think of Ben's sister as human. The little gargoyle had frozen

on the spot and Arabella had grabbed him.

Max took another step towards the window. He had to distract Arabella. The gargoyle chain must be ready by now.

"Cool!" he said suddenly, pointing towards the opposite corner of the room. "Look! There's a dear little mouse on the floor over there."

Arabella swung round to look. "A mouse!" she gasped. "I'd better pick it up before Fluffikins sees it."

She got down on her hands and knees and crawled into the corner.

Perfect! thought Max. He quickly undid the latch on the window and pushed it open wide.

"We've come to rescue you, Theo," he whispered.

To his surprise the kitten gave him a very cross glare. "Go away!" it mewed.

"I can't see a mouse." Arabella pouted as she stood up again. "Are you playing one of your silly tricks?"

Max rushed over to her side. "It was there, honest!" he exclaimed, pointing under a table. "I'm too clumsy to get it. You try. It probably won't be so scared of you."

Arabella dived under the table. Max glanced back at the window – just as Theo put out a determined paw and shut it!

As he did so there was a **thump** and Zack appeared, flattened against the pane of glass. He looked very surprised. The next minute he was whisked up out of sight and Max heard faint cackles of gargoyle laughter.

He zoomed out of the room, leaving Arabella under the table. He had to find his friends and work out a new plan.

When Max got back upstairs, Zack was sitting on the bed. His nose was bright red.

"Ssso much for the gargoyle chain," said
Eli. "Although it was fun hanging upside
down."

"Can we do it again?" asked Barney,
the spikes on his back
rippling hopefully.

"No!"
declared Zack,
rubbing his nose.

"I haven't
laughed so much
since we put pepper
in the vicar's hymn
book," said Toby.

"Trouble is," Max pointed
out, "Theo's having a
really good time.
He doesn't want
to be rescued!"

"He's been
brainwashed
by your sister,

Ben!" said Bart solemnly. "I think he's doomed."

"We don't seem to be cheering Bart up much," Max whispered to Ben. "He's gloomier than ever. And we can't start the sleepover without Theo."

"We'll soon change that," said Ben, "with my new plan." He dashed out of the room and was soon back carrying a furry toy cat. "Secret Plan: Swap the Cats. Agent Black, you distract Arabella. I'll grab Theo and put this toy cat in his place. It looks a bit like him."

"Stay here, gargoylz," said Max as they set off downstairs. "We'll soon have your friend back."

Ben put the toy cat behind his back and the two boys stepped boldly into the sitting room. Arabella was brushing Theo's coat. Theo seemed to be enjoying it. The boys stood there open-mouthed at the soppy scene.

"There wasn't a mouse," said Arabella
accusingly as soon as she saw them. "That
was a stupid trick, Max."

Max gulped. How was he going to
distract her this time? He'd have to talk
to her. And that meant girly chat! Yuck!
But he had to do it or Theo would be lost
for good.

"How could you think that dear little mouse was a trick?" he said, pretending to be hurt. "It was such a sweet little thing with its bright pink eyes and bright pink ... ears and everything ..."

Arabella sniffed crossly.

"... and you could have made such a cute little home for it," Max ploughed on in a yucky voice. He could see that Arabella's eyes now had a faraway look as she thought about this. "You could have called it 'Squeaky's Palace' ... or something sweet like that ..." He glanced over at Ben, wondering how long he was going to have to keep up this ghastly rubbish.

Then he heaved a sigh of relief. Ben
had made the switch and was already
halfway out of the room with Theo in
his arms. Max was just starting to follow
when Theo let out a loud, indignant
Meow!

"Fluffikins!" shrieked Arabella, startled
out of her daydream. "How dare you! Give
him back!" She snatched
Theo from Ben. "I'm
fed up with you two
and your tricks," she
snapped, throwing
the toy cat at the
boys. "Just go away
and don't come back!"

Theo looked extremely
smug as Arabella settled him back
down in his bed and launched into
a soothing lullaby.

"I can't believe it," said Ben, throwing the

toy cat onto the bed. "Theo doesn't even mind Arabella's dreadful singing. She'll be dressing him up next!"

"Spluttering gutterz!" declared Toby, flapping his wings in excitement. "That's given me an idea for the next plan. Find something really terrible that Theo would hate to wear, then tell your sister he'd love it. That should do the trick! Theo will be out of there before you can say whooshing waterspouts."

Ben looked at the toy cat. It was wearing a pink collar with sparkling diamond studs. "What about this!" he exclaimed, pulling it off and waving it in the air. "Secret Plan: Pink Horror."

"Just the thing!" chorused the gargoylz.

"Don't be surprised if he likes it," muttered Bart.

"Not you two again!" tutted Arabella in disgust as Ben and Max sidled into the sitting room once more.

"We've just come to say sorry," said Max. "Haven't we, Ben?"

Ben nodded. "And to give you something nice for your new kitten to wear." He held out the collar.

Arabella snatched it and inspected it suspiciously.

"No tricks," said Max solemnly. "It's just a nice sparkly collar – it'll look much better on your kitten than on that silly stuffed toy."

"It *is* very sweet," cooed Arabella, advancing on Theo, who was curled up in his rug, eyes closed. "Look what I've got here, Fluffikins." She dangled the collar in front of him.

Max and Ben held their breath.
At the sound of Arabella's voice
Theo woke up. Then he
saw the collar in her
hands. It sparkled
in the sunlight.
He leaped out of
his bed with a
horrified yowl
and raced around
the room.
Arabella chased
after him. "Come
back!" she shrieked,
knocking over vases and
scattering newspapers.
Max and Ben burst out
laughing – then stopped
abruptly as the sitting-room

door was flung open and
Ben's mum rushed in. Max
looked at Ben in horror.
How would they
ever rescue Theo now?
"What's going
on, Arabella?" she
demanded. "And
what is that kitten
doing here?"
"I found it up
next door's tree,"
panted Arabella,
making a dive for
Theo's tail. "I'm
looking after it."
"Take it back straight
away," said her mother.

"It's not yours and the neighbours will be missing it."

"But, Mum—" wailed Arabella.

"No arguments," said Mum firmly.

"Why don't Max and I take the kitten back?" suggested Ben. "We don't mind," he added, opening his blue eyes wide and looking helpful.

"That would be very kind." Mum smiled gratefully at the boys.

"You won't be able to catch him," said Arabella nastily.

Ben walked towards the kitten. Theo gave a meow and leaped into his arms. Ben smiled innocently and he and Max sped out of the door, leaving Arabella fuming.

The boys burst into the bedroom to a rousing cheer from the gargoylz, who gathered

around Theo as he wriggled back into his gargoyle shape.

"Thank you for rescuing me," he said. "I enjoyed being fussed over, but that collar was too much. If that's what kittens have to wear I'll never let myself get caught again!"

"Now that's all sorted out," said Ben, "we can get on with having fun."

Bart's ears pricked up. "Fun?" he said. "What sort of fun?"

Max winked at Ben. Bart was cheering up at last.

Max grinned. "Just you wait and see. This sleepover's going to be awesome."

4. Midnight Feast Fun

Max looked at his gargoyle friends, who were sitting in a row on Ben's bed, and grinned. "This is going to be the best sleepover ever!" he declared. "What shall we do first?"

"Cookiez and cake! Cookiez and cake!" shouted Zack, jumping up and down on the duvet.

"They're for later," Max told him. "Ben and I have only just had supper. Anyway, we have to eat them at midnight. That's why it's called a midnight feast."

"Let's play a game," suggested Ben.

"Good thinking, Agent Neal," said Max. "How about Twister?"

The gargoylz looked puzzled. Max got out a box and laid a big plastic sheet over the floor. On the sheet were different coloured circles.

Toby, Barney and Zack immediately leaped off the bed and jumped in and out of the circles.

Eli turned into a snake and slithered around, tripping them all up.

"Everyone off," laughed Ben. "The game hasn't started yet."

The gargoylz reluctantly stepped off the mat.

"Each time I call out a colour you all put one paw on a circle of that colour," explained Max. He spun an arrow on a card. "And this will tell you which paw. Look, put your front left paw on a red circle and keep it there." He spun again. "Now left back on a green circle. Last one to fall over wins. Eli, you need your paws so you'd better change back."

"Come and join in, Bart," said Ben. "It's a lot of fun."

"Certainly not," grumbled Bart. "Looks much too dangerous to me." And he hid his face in his gladiator skirt.

"Come on, Bart," said Zack, patting him on the back and knocking him off the bed.

"Just one game then," mumbled Bart.

Soon the mat was a tangle of scrambling gargoylz, with Bart in the middle, a big grin on his face.

"I'm winning!" Bart declared.

"That's because you're sitting on my wing," moaned Toby.

Suddenly they heard footsteps outside. The gargoylz dived under a chest of drawers just as Ben's mum stuck her head round the door.

"It's getting late, boys," she said, smiling. "No more jumping about. Time to settle down."

She went out again, closing the door. The gargoylz crawled out as Max and Ben quickly pulled on their pyjamas.

"Good game!" exclaimed Zack.

Bart nodded. "Very enjoyable. Especially as I won!"

"No you didn't," laughed Barney. "You pushed us all over!"

"Didn't!" said Bart.

"Did!" said all the other gargoylz.

"Shhhh!" warned Ben. "Mum'll hear."
He pulled out a lilo and began to blow it
up with a foot pump.

"What's that?" asked Theo, poking the
flabby plastic with his paw.

"It's Max's bed," said Ben.

The gargoylz immediately jumped
onto the lilo and rolled about as it
filled with air.

"There's only one thing wrong with this sssleepover," said Eli. "Ben's got his bed and Max has got the ssspare one. Where are *we* going to sssleep?"

"I hadn't thought of that," said Ben. "How about hanging off the windowsill? Or would you feel more at home dangling from the bookshelves?"

"But it's not a proper sssleepover if we don't have a bed like you," said Eli.

Ben ran to the cupboard. "I've got an idea," he grunted as he pulled a sleeping bag and a couple of pillows off the top shelf. "You can sleep in this. It should be big enough for you all."

He opened the sleeping bag up and folded it so that it looked like a bed, with the pillows arranged at the top. The gargoylz piled in excitedly.

"Move up, Zack," said Toby. "And stop those snakes wriggling about, Eli. They tickle. That's it – now we all fit."

Ben put his bedside light on and turned the main one off.

"This is so cosy," purred Theo. "Much better than that bed your sister made."

"Lovely," yawned Barney. "So comfortable . . ." His voice faded out and he fell asleep.

Toby nudged him. "You've got to stay awake for the midnight feast."

Barney jerked awake. "Sorry," he said, with his eyes half closed.

"We've got to do something to keep

him awake," Ben told Max. "It's ages till midnight."

"I've got a plan!" Max winked at him. "Let's tell a spooky story. No one can sleep through that."

"Brilliant, Agent Black," said Ben.

"Don't know any spooky stories," said Toby, looking puzzled. "Do we, gargoylz?" The others shook their heads.

"I know a good one," said Max. "Turn your light off, Ben. We need my multicoloured torch for this."

He sat down next to Ben. Then he shone his torch up under his chin, bathing his face in a ghostly green glow as he began his tale.

"Deep in the dark, dark wood lived a boy," he began in a creepy voice. "And

one dark, dark night he went out into the
dark, dark wood and—"

He stopped. There were footsteps on the
landing outside, getting nearer.

"Dangling drainpipes!" squeaked
Barney, his floppy ears pricked up with
fright. "It's something scary coming to
get us!"

"Worse than that," said Ben. "It's my
parents. They must be on their way to bed.
Quiet, everybody."

Max turned off his torch and they all
sat in the dark, listening as the footsteps
went past the door. The footsteps continued

into Ben's parents' bedroom and the door
closed. Max switched on the torch again.

"Where was I?" He grinned horribly in the torchlight.

"The dark, dark wood," said Theo in a tiny voice.

"Oh yes. The boy went out into the dark, dark wood and what did he see?"

The gargoylz' eyes grew wider and wider.

"A monster?" whispered Barney.

"A zombie?" quavered Eli, his snakes trembling.

"No," said Max. "He saw something white . . . and floaty . . . and it was coming towards him . . ."

"A ghost!" shrieked the gargoylz in terror.

"It was his friend under a sheet," Max laughed. "He'd dressed up to scare him!"

He shone his torch around the room. The gargoylz were lying in a trembling row, eyes like saucers, clutching the sleeping bag.

"All awake, I see," said Ben cheerfully.

"Wouldn't dare go to sleep after that story," whimpered Bart. "It was too scary."

Toby crawled up onto Ben's bed and gave Max a nudge. "I don't think scary stories are a good idea," he whispered. "Not if we want to cheer Bart up."

"You're right," said Max.

"How about telling jokes?" suggested Ben.

"Jokessssss?" Eli looked puzzled. He turned to Theo. "What are jokessss?"

"I don't know," Theo said with a shrug and the other gargoylz shook their heads.

"Jokes are very short, very funny stories," explained Max. "They're meant to make you laugh. Listen – why was the sand wet?"

"We don't know," said Zack. "Why *was* the sand wet?"

Max grinned. "Because the sea weed!"

"Seaweed?" The gargoylz looked at each other in bafflement.

 Then Toby burst out laughing. "The sea did a wee! That's what made the sand wet!" he explained to his friends. Soon they were all rolling around

on the floor holding
their sides. Even Bart
stopped looking scared
and managed a grin.

"We've got loads
more where that
came from," said Ben.
"What flies through the
air and wobbles?"

"I don't know,"
chorused the gargoylz, their eyes shining in
the torchlight.

"A jelly-copter!" giggled Ben.

"My turn," said Max. "Why didn't the
skeleton go to the party? Because he had
no*body* to go with!"

The gargoylz shook with laughter
in their little bed. Then they all heard
a strange noise. It was a wheezy, slurpy
sound like water draining down a rusty old
plughole. They looked in amazement to
see Bart holding onto his sides and rocking

backwards and forwards.

"Now I understand jokes," he spluttered. "Listen, I've got one. What do you call a pipe that rain runs along?"

"I don't know," said Ben. "What *do* you call a pipe that rain runs along?"

"A gutter!" chuckled Bart. The other gargoylz fell about laughing.

"That was the best one yet," wheezed Toby, tears of laughter running down his stony cheeks.

"Gutter!" repeated Zack, holding his sides.

Max looked at Ben. "Why is that funny?" he whispered.

"Beats me," said Ben. "I don't think Bart's quite got the hang of jokes yet."

"Well, at least it's cheered him up," Max said happily.

"Gutter!" Bart guffawed loudly, slapping his skirts.

"We'll have to keep the noise down," warned Ben. "My parents might hear – or worse, we might wake up my sister!"

The gargoylz all stopped laughing and looked horrified at the thought.

"Not Arabella!" Theo growled.

Max listened at the door. "It's OK," he said after a moment. "I think everyone's asleep. Time for the midnight feast!"

The gargoylz jumped up and down in excitement as Ben pulled out the bottle of fizzy drink and the chocolate cake.

"Cookiez first! Cookiez first!" chanted Zack, diving under the bed for the box.

Max took off the lid and

his face fell. "I might have known!" he exclaimed bitterly. "Look what my stupid sister's done with the icing."

The others peered into the box. All the cookies were bright girly pink – and decorated with sparkly icing stars and fairies. Some of them had writing on.

Max picked up the biggest cookie. "*Boys smell*," he read.

"Here's another one," said Toby. "*Boys are stupid*."

The gargoylz hooted with laughter.

"What do you call a boy with girly cookiez?" chortled Bart.

"I don't know," said Toby, his eyes bright with mischief.

"MAX!" crowed Bart.

The gargoylz rolled about their bed in delight.

Max took the cookie box and sat on his bed. "Well, if only girls eat pink cookies, then you lot won't be wanting any

and I've got them all to myself," he said
smugly, taking a big bite. "Delicious!" he
sighed.

"We didn't say we didn't want one," said
Barney, horrified. "I'm sure they're lovely."

"Yes." Toby nodded hurriedly. "Pink
cookiez are probably the best. We'd better
taste one to make sure."

Max grinned. "Go on then. Pass the
choccy cake, Ben."

For the next ten minutes the only
sound that could be heard was a happy
chomping and slurping. Bart made them
all giggle when the fizzy drink made him
burp and spiders came tumbling out of his
mouth.

Soon there were only a few cookies left.

"Dangling drainpipes!" said Toby, leaning back, his hands over his fat belly. "That was lovely."

"What do we do next on a sleepover?" asked Theo.

"Well, we could go to sleep, I suppose," said Ben.

"More jokes!" came Bart's gurgly voice.

"OK," said Ben. "Why did the ghost—"

"Quiet!" said Toby. "There are footsteps approaching."

"I can't hear anything," whispered Max, listening hard.

"Gargoylz have sssuper-sssensitive hearing," said Eli. "I can hear them too."

"Hide!" hissed Ben as he dived beneath his covers. Max jumped onto his bed. He heard the gargoylz scuttle under Ben's bed, dragging the cake tins with them. He suddenly remembered the drink. He grabbed the bottle, shoved it under his duvet and switched off the torch. And just in time.

The door to the bedroom was flung open and a figure stood there, outlined by the landing light. Max's radar burst into life: fluffy slippers, frilly nightdress, a look that could kill at ten paces. He knew what that meant. It was Enemy Agent Arabella Neal. Codename: Manic Monitor.

"Got you!" shouted Arabella. "You're mucking around and I'm telling. You're in big trouble and you deserve it after taking away my kitten. MUM! DAD!"

Footsteps could be heard running along the landing. Max knew he had to do something quickly. He had an idea. "What's going on?" he groaned as Ben's dad came into the room. Then he sat up and rubbed his eyes. "Why did you wake me up?"

Ben pretended he was still asleep. "I'm having a nightmare!" he wailed. "There's a monster in the doorway. It's got fluffy slippers and it's *sooo* ugly."

"Arabella!" Ben's dad sounded angry. "What are you doing out of bed?"

"The boys were—"

"Is this your idea of a joke?" growled Ben's dad. "The boys were fast asleep and you've woken them up. Go to bed – and I don't want to hear another peep out of you until morning."

Arabella stomped off.

"Sorry, boys," whispered Ben's dad. "Back to sleep now." He closed the door softly.

When it was safe, Max switched on the torch.

"There are still some cookies left," Ben said, peering into the tin. The gargoylz scrambled eagerly out from under the bed and tucked in.

"I haven't had such a tasty feast since I ate the vicar's holly bush," said Toby happily, wiping crumbs from his mouth.

"I've got another joke," declared Bart. "What did the cookie say when his friend was run over by a steamroller?"

"Tell us, Bart," said Max, exchanging a look with Ben. He could tell they were both wondering if it would be a real joke this time or another 'Bart Special'.

"He said, 'Oh, crumbs!'" said Bart proudly, a huge grin spreading over his face.

Max and Ben did a high-five as their gargoyle friends bounced around and laughed uproariously.

"Success, Agent Black," said Ben. "Not only have we outwitted Arabella and cheered up Bart, but he's got the hang of jokes!"

"Missions accomplished, Agent Neal," agreed Max. "This is officially the best sleepover in the history of sleepovers!"

Gargoylz Fact File

Full name: Tobias the Third
Known as: Toby
Special Power: Flying
Likes: All kinds of pranks and mischief
- especially playing jokes on the vicar
Dislikes: Mrs Hogsbottom, garden gnomes

Full name: Barnabas
Known as: Barney
Special Power: Making big stinks!
Likes: Cookiez
Dislikes: Being surprised by humanz

Full name: Eli
Special Power: Turning into
a grass snake
Likes: Sssports Day, sssslithering
Dislikes: Ssscary ssstories

Full name: Bartholomew

Known as: Bart

Special Power: Burping spiders

Likes: Being grumpy

Dislikes: Being told to cheer up

Full name: Theophilus

Known as: Theo

Special Power: Turning into a ferocious tiger (well, tabby kitten!)

Likes: Sunny spots and cosy places

Dislikes: Rain

Full name: Zackary

Known as: Zack

Special Power: Making himself invisible to humanz

Likes: Bouncing around, eating bramblz, thistlz, and anything with pricklz!

Dislikes: Keeping still

Full name: Ira
Special Power: Making it rain
Likes: Making humans walk the plank

Dislikes: Being bored

Name: Azzan
Special Power: Breathing fire

Likes: Surprises

Dislikes: Smoke going up
his nose and making him sneeze

The Gargoylz will return in

Gargoylz Take a Trip